Please, Puppy, Please

by Spike Lee & Tonya Lewis Lee

illustrations by Kadir Nelson

Simon & Schuster Books for Young Readers
New York   London   Toronto   Sydney

SIMON & SCHUSTER BOOKS FOR YOUNG READERS

An imprint of Simon & Schuster Children's Publishing Division

1230 Avenue of the Americas, New York, New York 10020

Text copyright © 2005 by Madstone, Inc. d/b/a Frecklestone

Illustrations copyright © 2005 by Kadir Nelson

All rights reserved, including the right of reproduction in whole or in part in any form.

SIMON & SCHUSTER BOOKS FOR YOUNG READERS is a trademark of Simon & Schuster, Inc.

Book design by Dan Potash

The text for this book is set in Imperfect Bold.

The illustrations for this book are rendered in oils.

Manufactured in China

ISBN 978-0-689-86804-7

0611 SCP

5 7 9 10 8 6 4

For Satchel, Jackson, and Ginger . . .

you are all doing just fine!

—T. L. L. and S. L.

For Amel and Aya, my little jitterbugs. Love, Daddy.

—K. N.

Stay inside today,
puppy puppy, please, puppy.

Outside? Let's go play,
puppy, puppy, puppy, please.

Away from the gate,
puppy puppy,
please, puppy.

Oh wait, **puppy**, wait,
please, please, please,
please.

Come back here! Don't go,
puppy puppy, **please**, puppy.

Not the mud, puppy. Oh no,
puppy, puppy, puppy,
please.

Rub-a-dub-dub,
plea**S**e, pl**e**ase,
puppy puppy?

Get back in the tub,

Puppy puppy puppy,

please!

Watch out for the cat,
puppy, please, puppy,
please!

Oh no, don't do that,
puppy puppy,
please, puppy!

Fetch me the ball,
puppy, puppy, puppy, please!

Come when I call,
puppy, please, please, please, please!

You're doing just fine,
**puppy puppy
puppy puppy.**

Always be mine,
puppy, please, puppy, please.